Compass Point

Phonics Readers

How a Frog Grows

by Celia Benton

Reading Consultant: Wiley Blevins, M.A.
Phonics/Early Reading Specialist

 COMPASS POINT BOOKS

Minneapolis, Minnesota

Compass Point Books
3109 West 50th Street, #115
Minneapolis, MN 55410

Visit Compass Point Books on the Internet at *www.compasspointbooks.com*
or e-mail your request to *custserv@compasspointbooks.com*

Photographs ©: Cover: DigitalVision, p. 1: DigitalVision, p. 6: Bruce Coleman, Inc./Jane
Burton, p. 7: Bruce Coleman, Inc./Robert Dunne, p. 8: Photo Researchers, Inc./Gary Meszaros,
p. 9: Bruce Coleman, Inc./Jane Burton, p. 10: Bruce Coleman, Inc./Kim Taylor, p. 11: Bruce
Coleman, Inc./Lee Rentz, p. 12: top left: Bruce Coleman, Inc./Jane Burton, p. 12: top right:
Bruce Coleman, Inc./Robert Dunne, p. 12: middle right: Photo Researchers, Inc./Gary
Meszaros, p. 12: bottom: Bruce Coleman, Inc./Jane Burton, p. 12: middle left: DigitalVision

Editorial Development: Alice Dickstein, Alice Boynton
Photo Researcher: Wanda Winch
Design/Page Production: Silver Editions, Inc.

Library of Congress Cataloging-in-Publication Data
Benton, Celia.
  How a frog grows / by Celia Benton.
      p. cm. — (Compass Point phonics readers)
  Summary: Briefly describes the life cycle of a frog, in a text that
  incorporates phonics instruction.
  Includes bibliographical references (p. 16).
    ISBN 0-7565-0509-7 (hardcover : alk. paper)
  1. Frogs—Life cycles—Juvenile literature. 2. Reading—Phonetic
  method—Juvenile literature. [1. Frogs. 2. Tadpoles. 3.
  Reading—Phonetic method.] I. Title. II. Series.
    QL668.E2B44 2003
    597.8—dc21   2003006353

Table of Contents

Parent Letter **4**

"Mary Had a Little Lamb" **5**

How a Frog Grows **6**

Word List **13**

Batter Up! **14**

Read More **16**

Index **16**

Dear Parent or Caregiver,

Welcome to Compass Point Phonics Readers, books of information for young children. Each book concentrates on specific phonic sounds and words commonly found in beginning reading materials. Featuring eye-catching photographs, every book explores a single science or social studies concept that is sure to grab a child's interest.

So snuggle up with your child, and let's begin. Start by reading aloud the Mother Goose nursery rhyme on the next page. As you read, stress the words in dark type. These are the words that contain the phonic sounds featured in this book. After several readings, pause before the rhyming words, and let your child chime in.

Now let's read *How a Frog Grows.* If your child is a beginning reader, have him or her first read it silently. Then ask your child to read it aloud. For children who are not yet reading, read the book aloud as you run your finger under the words. Ask your child to imitate, or "echo," what he or she has just heard.

Discussing the book's content with your child:
Explain to your child that many frogs have sticky tongues, which flick out to catch passing insects. Other frogs leap out of the water to catch prey. Frogs eat huge numbers of insects, which might otherwise destroy crops and other plants.

At the back of the book is a fun Batter Up! game. Your child will take pride in demonstrating his or her mastery of the phonic sounds and the high-frequency words.

Enjoy Compass Point Phonics Readers and watch your child read and learn!

Mary Had a Little Lamb

Mary had a little lamb,
Its fleece was white as **snow;**
And everywhere that Mary went,
The lamb was sure to **go.**

It followed her to school one day,
That was against the rule;
It made the children laugh and play,
To see a lamb in school.

A frog lays its eggs in water.
A frog egg is small.
It is as small as this dot!   .

A tadpole grows from an egg.
A tadpole has a tail to swim with.
It has gills to breathe in water.
It looks like a fish, not a frog!

The tadpole begins to change.
It grows back legs.
It grows lungs.
Now it needs air to breathe.

The tadpole grows and changes.
Front legs grow.
The tail shrinks.
At last, the tadpole is a frog.

The frog can go live on land now.
It has lungs to breathe air.
It can leap to get food.
"Croak," comes from its throat.

The frog grows and grows.
The grown frog will lay eggs.
What will grow from the eggs?
Tadpoles!

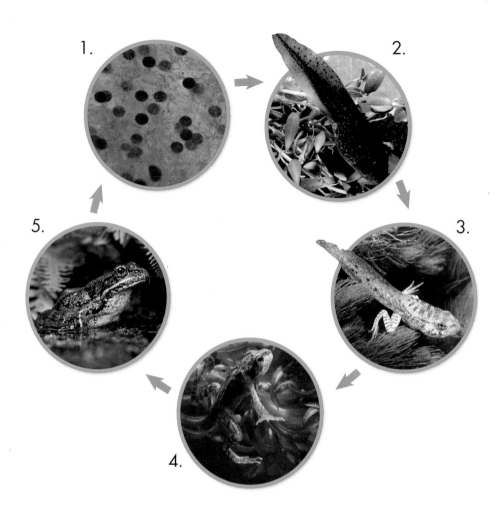

This is how a frog grows.
Tell about it.

Word List

Long *o (o, oa, ow)*

o
go

oa
croak
throat

ow
grow(s)
grown

Digraphs
breathe
change(s)
fish

shrinks
the
this
throat
what
with

High-Frequency
comes
now

Science
air
lungs
water

Batter Up!

You will need:
- 1 penny
- 2 moving pieces, such as nickels or checkers

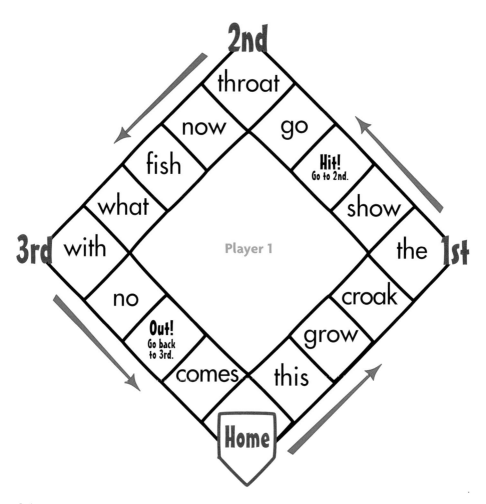

2nd

throat

now   go

fish   Hit! Go to 2nd.

what   show

3rd with   Player 1   the 1st

no   croak

Out! Go back to 3rd.   grow

comes   this

Home

14

How to Play

- Put the moving pieces on Home. The first player shakes the penny and drops it on the table. Heads means move 1 space. Tails means move 2 spaces.
- The player moves and reads the word. If the child does not read the word correctly, tell him or her what it is. On the next turn, the child must read the word before moving.
- A run is scored by the first player to arrive at Home plate, and the inning is over. Continue playing out the number of innings previously decided. The player with the most runs wins.

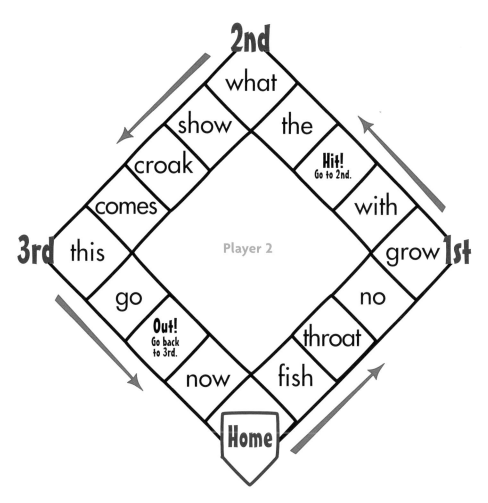

Read More

Arnosky, Jim. *All About Frogs.* New York: Scholastic, 2002.

Cowley, Joy, and Nic Bishop (photographer). *Red-Eyed Tree Frog.* New York: Scholastic Press, 1999.

Heinrichs, Ann. *Frogs.* Nature's Friends Series. Minneapolis, Minn.: Compass Point Books, 2003.

Trumbauer, Lisa. *The Life Cycle of a Frog.* Mankato, Minn.: Pebble Books, 2002.

Index

air, 8, 10

egg(s), 6, 7, 11

fish, 7

frog, 6, 7, 9, 10, 11, 12

gills, 7

grow(s), 7, 8, 9, 11, 12

leap, 10

legs, 8, 9

lungs, 8, 10

small, 6

tadpole(s), 7, 8, 9, 11

tail, 7, 9

throat, 10

water, 6, 7